MOTHER'S FINEST

NAPOLEON ESTEBAN

Books Academy LLC
112 SW H K Dodgen Loop, Temple, Texas 76504
Hotline: (254) 800-1189

Ordering Information:
Quantity sales. Special discounts are available on quantity purchases by corporations, associations, and others. For details, contact the publisher at the address above.

Printed in the United States of America.

ISBN-13:　　Softcover　　978-1-966567-81-3
　　　　　　eBook　　978-1-966567-82-0
　　　　　　Hardback　　978-1-966567-83-7

Library of Congress Control Number: 2025911997

ESTEBAN

INTRODUCTION

Ah, you've made it. Come in. Don't mind the smell — it's just a little ego decomposing in the corner.

Welcome to Mother's Finest, a lovingly curated collection of those who lived beautiful lives and died slightly more... expressive deaths. You'll find no heroes here, no saints — just cheekbones, charm, and an unshakable belief that youth is forever.
Spoiler: it's not.

I'll be your guide as we tour the once-glorious. Each illustration in these pages captures a moment after the mirror cracked — when time caught up with beauty and whispered, "Now it's my turn." The stories? Think of them as eulogies with a bite — testimonies to vanity's last stand before rigor mortis set in.

These zombies don't moan for brains. They crave attention. They still believe they're being photographed. And in a way, they are — preserved here, forever, as cautionary tales in couture.

So fix your hair, check your teeth, and take a stroll through what's left of the best-looking corpses you've ever seen.

We begin with the one who thought she was too flawless to die.

Shall we?

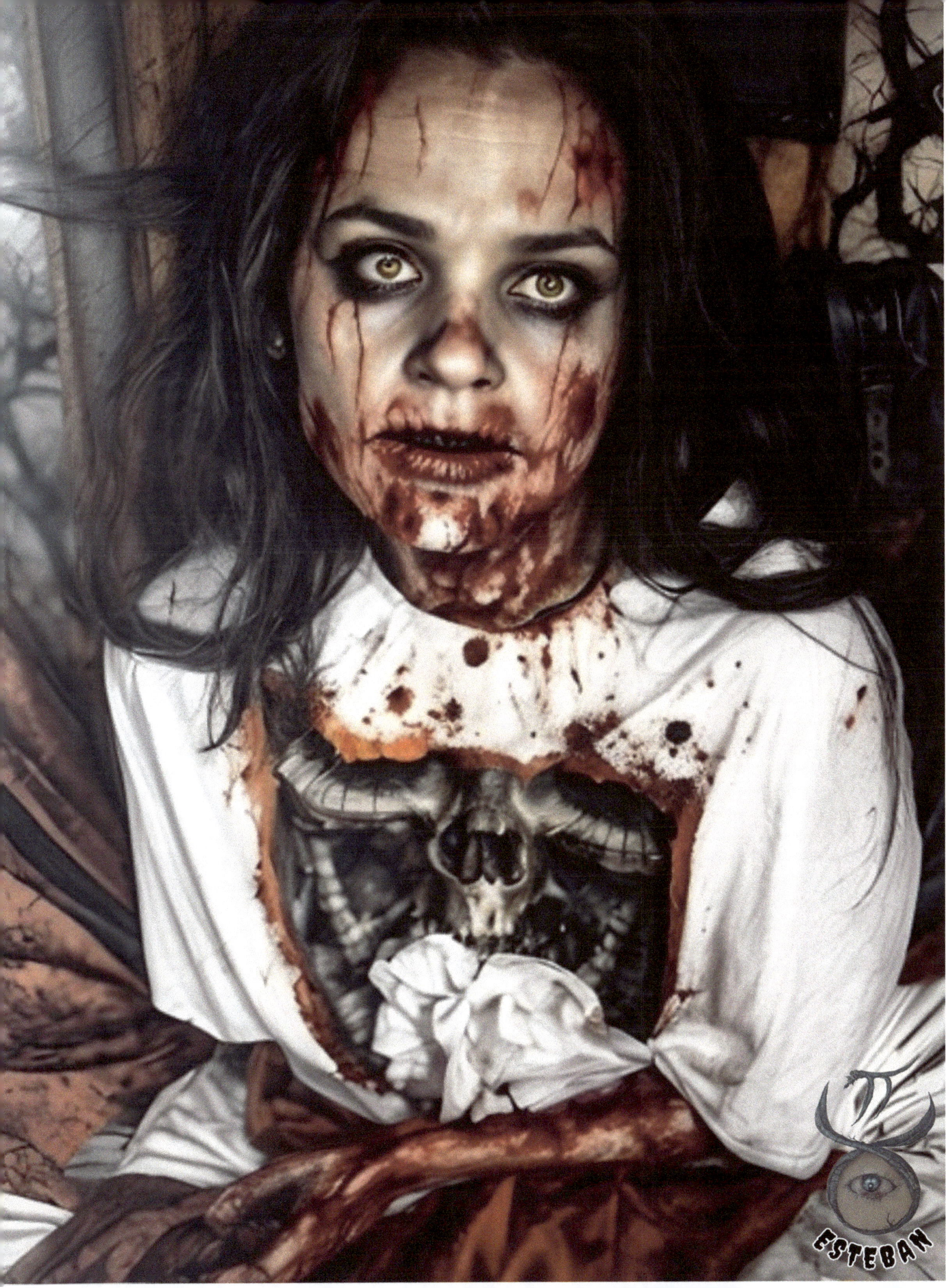

ESTEBAN

Dani was born beautiful. With her lovely complexion and long, thick black hair, she had no problem attracting attention. At times, it became too much for her.

"Do people like me for who I am, or for what I look like?" she would constantly ask herself.

Unfortunately, over time, she grew numb to the question and began exploiting her appearance. People didn't care about who she was — they only wanted to be associated with her, hoping it might open doors for them.

Always in the limelight, Dani lost her way. Taking advantage of others became her norm. She began to think of herself as God's gift to the world. Fueled by ego and unrealistic expectations, she believed she was living a fabulous life with no end in sight.

Mirror, mirror, on the wall always reassured her of her beauty.

Until, one day, it didn't.

Her eye began to droop — a lazy eye, the doctors said. Then came a skin condition that dulled and damaged her once-perfect complexion. And if that wasn't enough, her hair grew knotted and tangled, eventually falling out.

The one thing she had counted on to sustain her — her looks — was now abandoning her.

All the attention she craved was redirected to others. Left alone, she returned to the question she once asked:

Do people like me for who I am, or for what they see?

I'm sure she got the right answer.

ZLALIWEWEE
ESTEB

Zarita was truly a stunning young woman from Italy. Not only was she incredibly attractive, but she was also highly intelligent. Sophisticated and cultured, she spoke four languages fluently.

Her dream? To become an international model and actress.

As we all know, reaching our goals requires focus and discipline. Dreams don't come true overnight — there are steps, sacrifices, and structure.

But Zarita thought she was an exception.

She believed she was so special that discipline didn't apply to her. In her mind, all she had to do was snap her fingers and success would appear.
Spoiler: it didn't.

Although she had both beauty and brains, she chose to use them in the ugliest way possible. Instead of pursuing her dreams, she decided she'd be better off as a con artist.

And she was good at it.

She perfected the craft — living in a luxury condo, driving a high-end car, and flaunting a wardrobe to die for. All without working a single day in her life. She was so confident, so smug, convinced that her schemes would never catch up with her.

But when you think you're smarter than everyone else... eventually, you outsmart yourself.

Zarita became the victim of a bigger scam than her own. Her entire world — every stolen luxury — was stripped away, leaving her to rot in the aftermath of her own deceit.

She died in prison.

Alone, forgotten, and no longer so stunning.

ESTEBAN

Malignant narcissism — that's the only way to describe Danee.

Once again, we meet a beautiful woman who believed she was entitled to everything others had worked for. But Danee wasn't just vain — she was dangerous.

She's the kind of person you should never let into your home, let alone your life. Cunning and manipulative barely scratch the surface. She would literally bite the hands that fed her — and then convince everyone you were the villain.

She had no conscience. No remorse. No sense of right or wrong. One minute, she was preaching the Word — the next, she was wielding it like a weapon.

Yes, she had the credentials — a bachelor's in Teaching and a law degree from a prestigious university. But no diploma could save her from the disorder inside her mind.

Even her own family couldn't stand her — worn down by her need to control, dominate, and destroy. She didn't just burn bridges. She torched entire towns.

Her mind turned on itself.
And now?

She wears a straitjacket in a mental institution, where every day she watches her beauty fade and her brilliance unravel.

So much potential.

Such a waste.

She simply couldn't get out of her own way.

There are some cultures in this world who believe that each time a camera takes your photograph, it captures a part of your soul. If this is true, then there must be many soulless people in the world.

Leah, would certainly fall in this population. I never met her in person. The only way I knew her was through the hundreds of photos she would share. At first, I was pleased at her sharing but, as time went on, there was no relationship or any potential relationship.

She did not appear to be able to hold a conversation. She never attempted to know anything about me or share anything personal about herself. Her photos had lost their value. I could not look at them anymore.

Had she become so involved with her relationship with the camera that she lost her soul? I don't know. I only know what she had shown me, and it wasn't promising.

There's nothing wrong with being attractive, but you shouldn't let it go to your head. She thought the way to a man's heart was through his eyes.

As she aged and found herself alone, her interest in taking photos of herself faded. She no longer saw her beauty as a re-lationship factor. Her only relationship had been between her and the camera.

ESTEB

Dark Spaces — for the home you'd kill to die in.

Our interior designers specialize in creating hauntingly beautiful spaces that leave family, friends, and unexpected guests utterly envious. Our buyers scour the globe for the most unique furniture and accessories — each piece curated to make your home stand out... in the eeriest way possible.

And don't worry about the cost — we offer a one-of-a-kind financing program with interest rates so low, it's almost scary.

Our sales?

Out of this world. Especially in October.

We were recently featured in the ever-popular magazine Better Horrors and Goblins, where we were recognized for our killer merchandise and undying customer service.

So if your crypt — sorry, home — needs a makeover, come visit us.

You'll find us at:
666 Spirit Drive
Hadesville, Georgia

Where style meets the afterlife.

HALLWEEN
ZOMBIE
HALLOWEEN
ESTEB

Look at me now.

You'd never believe that my face was once plastered all over the world.

There wasn't a place I could go without being recognized. Things got so intense, I had to hire a body double just to distract the crowds desperate to catch a glimpse of me.

Yes, there was a time when I was considered one of the most beautiful and sexiest women in the world. I had fulfilled my dream, and

I couldn't have been happier.

I always knew I was special — and I wanted to share myself with the world.

I was never ashamed to pose nude. I wanted everyone to see how voluptuous and sensual I was. I loved the way they worshipped me.

But little did I realize: what goes up, must eventually come down.

The adoration from the crowds gave me so much joy, and I never wanted it to end — until I had to increase my security.

Not all my fans were really fans. Many were little more than psychotic stalkers, obsessed and fantasizing about God knows what.

Before I knew it, the high that came with fame turned into paranoia. I became afraid to go outside.

Doctors gave me prescriptions meant to help… but they only led to addiction.

I was becoming a hot mess.

I hate being famous. Because at the end of the road, you don't go out gracefully — you go up in flames.

Look at me now.

Do you still dream about sharing a life with me?

All that glitters isn't gold.

ESTEBAN

"Momma told me not to come."

Hi everyone, my name is Bella, and I'm happy to spend this time with you. Out of all those competing, my boss chose me to represent his domain. What an honor.

My story? It's all about me — and if you listen closely, you just might learn something. I was the middle child of twelve, raised in a strict religious household. My father was even a pastor for a time. I think that's what made me so rebellious. Whenever my mother told me not to do something, I did just the opposite. I was convinced she didn't know what she was talking about. I was the prettiest of the girls, and I thought that meant I could do whatever I wanted. I wasn't interested in school or a career — I just wanted a man. And I had plenty of them.

During my early wild days, I gave birth to twelve children by nine different men.

After having my first two daughters, I met a man. We got married and had two sons. While I was still married, I met another man, got pregnant by him, and had another son — but I gave that child my husband's name. I was just getting started.

Then I met another man and had two daughters with him, giving them his name.

After that, I met yet another man. We had a son and a daughter, but I went back to giving them my husband's name. Mind you, their father lived in the home with us — yet wasn't man enough to claim them. While living with this so-called man, I met someone else. We had a daughter. And yes, I gave her my husband's name too.

My husband would've been shocked to know how many children carried his name.

Still not done.

After having that daughter, I was still living with the previous man — the one who fathered two of my children. He and I had another daughter together. And of course… I named her after my husband too. So my first two sons ended up sharing their father's name with five other children — bastards, fathered by three different men. Isn't that enough for a free ticket to hell?

I lived to be eighty-eight and witnessed the curses that came from my womb. When I died, I found myself back in the super fine body of my youth. I could hardly believe it! Whatever this place was, it looked like Heaven. All my friends were there. So were all the men I had ever been with.

But then… I looked in the mirror. That's when I realized I was far from Heaven. My beautiful body was decaying right before my eyes. The worst part? I had to watch it decay — for eternity.

And that's all, folks

If I could go back in time, I would do whatever I could to pre-vent this nightmarish life. All the while I thought I was on top of the world... I was actually in a downward spiral. I've been falling into a bottomless pit — and there's no end in sight.

During this endless descent, I'm forced to face everything I did in my life — the good, the bad, and the ugly.

And it seems the bad outweighs the good by a long shot.
Was there a way to live that could have spared me this fate?
Yes, I knew the difference between right and wrong.

But my beauty and youth made me reckless. I threw caution to the wind.

I lived for the moment — and the moment always demanded more.

The alcohol, the drugs, the wild parties, the unprotected sex — with both boys and girls — these were the things that dominated my life.

Hell — excuse me, heck — I was a cool, liberal woman just following the crowd.
You know the old saying: "If it feels good, do it."
Well... it felt good.
And I did it.

They say we only live once.
But no one ever tells you what comes after.

When is life really over?
How far do I have to fall before I finally hit the bottom?

ESTEBAN

Hi, my name is Rosita, and I live in the Dominican Republic. It's a beautiful place, especially for tourists. But for those of us who live here permanently, life can be challenging. Although the government has created various programs to support young women like me, many of us have found an easier way to improve our lives.

Thanks to the internet, dating apps, and money transfer services, we've discovered how to make money without traditional work. We are attractive, confident women who are willing to show our bodies. We've realized that American and Canadian men are drawn to exotic island girls—and they often have money to spend.

All we have to do is get their attention by sending sexually explicit photos and videos. Honestly, it's like taking candy from a baby. The key is to make them feel like we're genuinely interested in them.

This line of work has helped me a lot. I've received thousands of dollars, which I've used for groceries, rent, utilities, furniture, and even appliances. I thank God for the internet!

I also want to give a big shout-out to WhatsApp. Thanks to their focus on privacy, we can send our clients content that only gynecologists usually see.

The only downside is that as we get older, our bodies change and our beauty fades. So I highly recommend that young women take full advantage of their youth—and get that money while you can!

ESTE

I never had a love to call my own,
I was about to give up——until you came along.
Just to have your tender ways
Thrilled me for days and days.
I don't care what nobody says,

I want you for always.
Now that I have found you, I want to stay around you——
So, make me yours.

You've already taken my heart and my soul;
Now I'm begging you to take full control.
I need the love that only you can give.
If I can't have it, I don't want to live.

Artist unknown

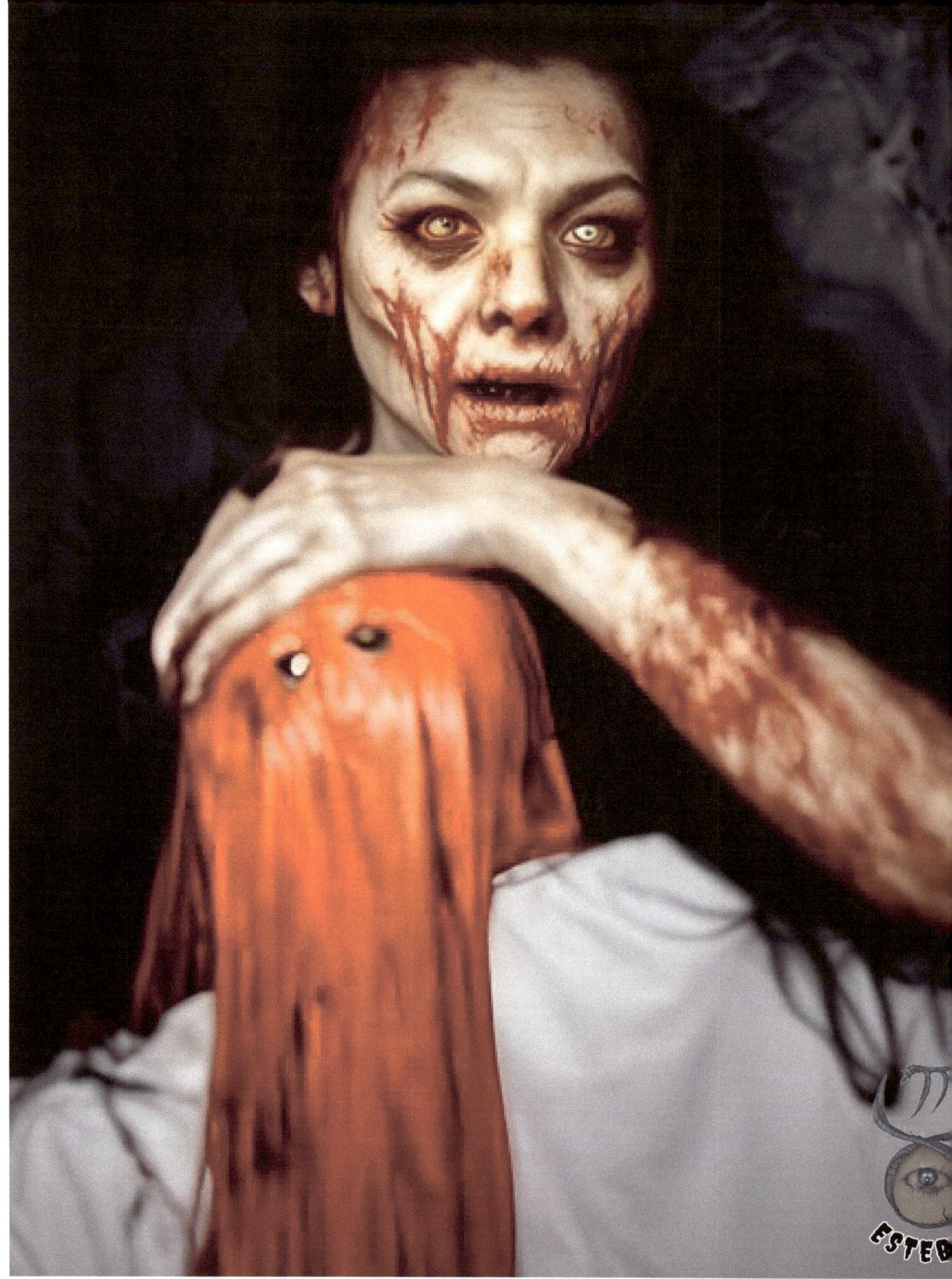

ESTEB

Through these eyes, I see my life leaving my body and traveling to another realm. In this place, there is no space or time, yet I still exist. I am not alone——I am surrounded by legions of unfamiliar spirits. Some are here to offer comfort, while others are here to torment.

I must be careful of the spirit of deception, which makes it difficult to tell who is genuine. I find myself confused, unsure of which direction to take. But in this realm, I realize, no direction exists.

There is no up or down, no east or west, no right or wrong. All I know is that I exist. My thoughts are without words and have no meaning. How did I get here?

I am never tired or hungry, nor do I feel emotions that affect my mind. I don't look forward to or dread tomorrow. Without time, yesterday, today, and tomorrow have no relevance. I have no need for knowledge. I am obsolete.

RASPUTIN'S BAR AND GRILL

WHERE THE PARTY PEOPLE MEET FOR A GOOD TIME

YOU'RE NEVER A STRANGER HERE!

HAPPY HOUR NEVER ENDS

UPBEAT MUSIC KEEPS THE DANCE FLOOR JUMPING

BEST FOOD AND DRINKS IN TOWN

LARGE SPECIALTY PIZZA, CALZONES, SIRLOIN STEAK, SALAD BAR, BUFFALO CHICKEN, BARBEQUE RIBS, PHILLY CHEESESTEAK, STROMBOLI, AND A WIDE SELECTION OF APPETIZERS AND DESSERTS

NO NEED FOR RESERVATIONS, JUST GET HERE WHEN YOU CAN!

187 GULFLINKS DRIVE, MIAMI, FLORIDA

ZOMBE
ZOMBE
ESTEB

BE ALL THAT YOU CAN BE

JOIN THE ARMY AND SEE WHAT YOU'VE BEEN MISSING

TRAVEL THE WORLD

GREAT EDUCATIONAL BENEFITS

UPWARD MOBILITY OPPORTUNITIES

BE ON A TEAM OF WINNERS

YOU'LL SEE WHY OUR RECRUITMENT IS STEADILY INCREASING

DO YOUR PART TO KEEP OUR COUNTRY STRONG

CONTACT YOUR LOCAL RECRUITMENT OFFICE TODAY!

ESTEV

My name is Shinobu, and I lived in Japan. There were many U.S. military installations in my country, and I was always interested in meeting an American. Although I was born on the southern tip of Japan, as I grew older, I moved to places where I could meet and marry the man of my dreams.

I consider myself attractive, but I am also very creative and independent. I was never looking for someone to take care of me——I have always been in control of my life. That changed the day I met the man I eventually married.

At first, he was kind and loving. He made me feel special. Unfortunately, as time passed, he changed. This caused me to question what love really meant. To cope with my husband's loss of affection, I began drinking and taking pills. It was a poor decision, and I quickly found myself spiraling out of control.

We ended up getting divorced, and he returned to the United States. Alone, my drinking and drug use increased, which impaired my judgment and led me to make many mistakes. I kept meeting the wrong kind of men.

My friends tried to help me, but I was determined to destroy my own life. I became afraid of anything that looked promising. I developed a pessimistic view of life and no longer wanted any lightness. I became my worst enemy.

I didn't take my life——I let my lifestyle slowly drain it from me. It's sad that I allowed another person to have such a powerful impact on me. I wasn't wrong to love him; I was wrong for not loving myself.

ESTEBAN

Esteban, Where Did You Go?

My name is Meila, and I live in Bogotá, Colombia. I'm a successful fashion designer. I love jazz, dancing, and nature. I met Esteban about three years ago. He told me I was very attractive and wanted to get to know me.

He expressed himself so eloquently that it wasn't long before I found myself falling for him. He said he had photos of me all over his home——that I was the first thing he saw when he woke up each morning, and that he thought about me every day.

I had never met a man like him. He made me feel very special. I always looked forward to hearing from him. But now, for some reason, I rarely hear from him. My heart feels empty. Did he find someone else to take my place? If so, he should have told me instead of keeping me hanging on.

I truly miss him and would love to hear him say that he misses me too. I don't believe in soul mates. The idea that there's just one person meant for me doesn't make sense. The person who is truly compatible is the one who steps up to the plate and commits. That person must be wise enough to accept the other without trying to change them.

Most importantly, each should enhance the other's life. Nothing lasts forever. However, we should be stronger for the experience and celebrate the time we shared.

One thing I don't understand is that Esteban would always tell me how beautiful I was—so why does he depict me as a zombie? Could it be that he's afraid of his feelings for me and tries to destroy how he really sees me?

I'm not a psychologist, and I don't have the expertise to figure out how this man thinks. Hopefully, someday he'll explain it all to me. In the meantime, I'll continue to live my best life.

ESTEB

Lady of the Island

The brownness of her body glowed in the firelight—except for the places where the sun refused to reach. Our bodies were a perfect fit, and afterward, we lay together in quiet contentment.

Kazuwa was a beautiful soul who worshiped the sun. Every day, she would retreat to her isolated spot on the island, lie nude on the white sand, and let the sun bathe her body. I often called her my Golden Goddess.

Some of my most pleasant memories are the times we shared at her secret place. We didn't want those moments to end. Unfortunately, circumstances forced me to move on without her. She pleaded with me to stay on the island with her.

As I left, she whispered a soft goodbye and told me she would never leave her secret place. She preferred to lie in the sun, holding onto the memories of our time together.

But the sun's rays eventually baked her skin beyond repair. She became a casualty of the very thing she loved.

Jill
LEON ESTEBAN

Fried Zucchini

Jenna had all the makings of an All-American girl. She came from a loving and supportive family that encouraged her aspirations. She wanted to be a photojournalist and cover social issues, and she graduated from a private university that prepared her for her future endeavors.

Jenna was attractive, intelligent, and held strong moral values. However, she was naïve. After graduating, she met a charismatic man who convinced her to work at his community center. Little did she know that she would become part of his harem. This man's name was Lucifer.

Lucifer targeted young women who had graduated from her university, using their educational backgrounds to develop his community center. He also exploited them sexually, making each of them believe that they were special.

Lucifer controlled them to the point that he had a key to their apartments and would enter their homes whenever he pleased. These young women became nothing more than his property.

Lucifer invited one of his relatives to join the community center staff. This relative was an artist who also enjoyed writing. It wasn't long before he and Jenna became friends. They began spending time together after work, going to her apartment where they had great conversations, drank wine, listened to her music, and enjoyed her favorite fried zucchini.

They developed a good relationship without any intimacy involved. There may have been some desire, but she already belonged to Lucifer. This was made clear one evening when they were enjoying each other's company, and Lucifer unlocked the door to her apartment, entered one of the rooms as if he were looking for something, and then left. This was certainly his way of asserting, "This is my property."

Despite this, they continued to see each other. One night, the conditions were right for them to take their relationship to another level. Without going into details, it was a memorable night. However, Jenna's conscience soon troubled her.

She had been intimate with two cousins whom she worked with and saw every day. She considered herself a good, decent woman. How could she have let this happen?

Lucifer's cousin felt that their intimacy had consummated their relationship. Jenna told him it had been a mistake and that it could never happen again since she belonged to Lucifer. Although the cousin tried to accept her decision, the work environment made it difficult for him to stay.

Who knows what else Jenna did while serving Lucifer? Most likely, she will take this secret to her grave.

ESTEBAN

Lucifer — Speaking of the devil, there he is. Cunning, manipulative, controlling, and downright a crook. Yes, he may be charismatic, but it's all part of his strategy. He wants your soul, and if you have any money, he wants that too.

There are so many examples of this demon's history that it could fill a book all by itself. To sum things up, he can be described as a classic corrupted spirit.

Let us come together in one accord. Let us praise and give thanks to our Lord. Let us bow our heads; everyone, come on board. If you don't, I'll chop your head off with my mighty sword. I represent God's word; He directs my path. When you see me, you will also see God.

We need to be very careful about claiming that God told us to do something. There are times when we make God look bad. People often say, "God told me to do this," or "God told me to do that." What a blessing it must be that God speaks directly to you!

Some individuals go to others to say, "God told me to tell you." To those people, I say, "Get behind me." In most cases, it's nothing more than their ego seeking attention.

Organized religion can be intimidating and often equates to a hierarchy of the flesh.

Don't you dare say anything negative about my pastor. Everything that comes out of his mouth is the Gospel. You all need to praise and worship your pastor. And the pastor says, "Amen to that."

There are only two kinds of pastors: God's anointed and those who are self-appointed.

Faith versus Logic — Let's say you run out of gas while driving down the highway. What would be more effective: praying over the car or getting a ride to the gas station to get some gas?

I knew a man of faith who was asked to leave the military for a pastoral position. This man made his decision based on the income being commensurate with what he was receiving in the military.

The Pope is elected by his peers.

Hey everyone, my name is John Doe, and I'm on my way to church! What does that even mean? Who am I trying to impress? Look at me——I'm a good man. A good man doesn't need recognition.

"What church do you belong to?"
"Oh, my church is better than yours."

Don't call on the pastor if you need help——if there's nothing in it for her, forget about it.

The church is supposed to be a spiritual hospital. But if you're having marital problems, substance abuse issues, financial struggles, or even contemplating suicide, don't expect to be welcomed in.

"Woe be unto the pastors that destroy and scatter the sheep of my pasture! saith the Lord." —— Jeremiah 23:1

ESTEB

Jamison's Curse. I was adopted by Timothy and Penny Daniels. At least, that's who I thought they were. Adoption agencies have a responsibility to perform some fact-finding before approving an adoption.

My adopted father was not really a Daniels. His mother got pregnant by someone who was not her husband. She couldn't remember the man's name, so she conveniently gave a false name. At the time, she was married to George W. Daniels, and they had two sons, George Jr. and Stephen Mott.

The mother did not identify the father on the birth certificate. She knew George Daniels was not Timothy's biological father. She let this lie continue until Timothy obtained a copy of his birth certificate and saw the father's name was left blank. Who is this man? What is his real name?

I guess it was common practice among some mothers back then. I found out my adopted mother's maiden name was Stevens—not Stevens, but actually Bowen. My adopted parents were bastard children whose mothers wrongly gave their husbands' names to them.

If this information had been disclosed to the adoption agency, maybe the adoption wouldn't have been approved.

George Jr. died in Vietnam at the tender age of twenty. Stephen was the only remaining Daniels son. He and my adopted father were very different, and I always thought highly of Stephen.

Even though he lived in San Antonio, Texas, the rest of the siblings depended on him to take care of their mother. After her husband died, no one——including my adopted father——cared about her welfare.

I was shocked to learn Timothy was not the only child who was wrongly named. Five of her other children were named Daniels, but they had three different fathers! I understand Stephen's displeasure at sharing the Daniels name under such shameful circumstances.

For some reason, after they didn't need Stephen anymore, they cut him off from the family and sabotaged his relationship with their mother. Timothy claimed he was the oldest, knowing full well there was no Daniels blood in his veins.

This is where my problem began. Not understanding the real issues between half-brothers, I was dead wrong to say anything. I was angry to think that if my adopted father isn't really a Daniels, then I had inherited a lie——a lie I passed on to my wife and my future children.

I told Stephen Mott Daniels to f——k off. My adopted father, whoever he really is, was not man enough to correct me. I made that statement because I was wrong. I don't really know Stephen Mott Daniels, Sr., yet I cursed him out——and I gave my children his name. How cool is that?

ESTEBAN

Spirits in the Dream

Have you ever had a dream like this? Can't quite make out its meaning, if it has any meaning at all.

Some dreams make you wake up screaming, afraid to go back to sleep.

Have you ever had one of those dreams where something is chasing you? You run and run, but it's right behind you. Look out! It's got you.

Gold and rose—the colors of the dream I had not too long ago. Misty blue and violet too, colors that never grow old.

These dreams appear when I close my eyes. Are they real? Another dimension of our reality?

Have you ever met people in your dreams you've never met before? Who are they, and what do they want?

What about recurring dreams? Have you ever dreamed of being naked in public? How often do you dream like that? Are you trying to find something to cover yourself, or do you just walk around naked?

What about those dreams when you're falling… falling… falling? What happens if you hit the ground before you wake up?

Do you look forward to your dreams?

What would you consider to be a nightmare? When was your last nightmare?

Have your dreams ever felt physical?

The Council on Life

Imagine these men observing you to determine your fate. Do you trust them? What criteria will they use before passing judgment? Will they be biased or impartial?

Who is in the right position to determine another's fate? If they swear before God, does that make them credible?

These men accused me of doing a terrible thing, which I was innocent of. However, my response to this council was, "I may not be guilty of your accusation, but I know I'm guilty of much worse."

They looked at each other in confusion, then turned to me and told me I was excused.

Whenever a person wants out of a commitment, they start looking for a reason.

I only wanted to live in accordance with the prompts that came from my true self. Why would that be so difficult? —— Herman Hesse

Is it better to travel hopefully than to arrive?

"There is a way which seemeth right unto a man, but the end thereof are the ways of death." —— Proverbs 14:12

ESTEB

Why celebrate Halloween on just one day instead of all year long? We wear different masks every day to hide our true selves. Over time, we forget who we really are.

What is it about this day that makes people so excited? Is it because they can be who they truly are without fear of judgment?

We're all lost in a masquerade.

So we run—and run—to keep up with the sun, but it's sinking. Chasing around just to come up behind us again. It's always the same, in a relative way, and we're all out of breath, one day closer to death. —— Pink Floyd

ESTEB
ESTEB

I thought I did everything right.

Nettie met a man she believed she had fallen in love with. Although she was married, she withheld that information. Once she discovered she was pregnant, she told her new man and divorced her husband.

If it doesn't start right, it won't end right.

She and her new husband got married and bought a new home two months before the child was born. They had a beautiful son, named after his father. As time passed, everything seemed fine. The young family appeared blessed.

The relationship between father and son was very strong. The father fully participated in nurturing his child. Nettie often told him he was the better parent. The father felt he was simply fulfilling his responsibilities and loving his son.

Nettie liked to read romance novels and fantasize about an ideal relationship. Even though she loved her husband and often told him what a good man he was, deep inside she wasn't happy. She wanted Prince Charming to come into her life and rescue her.

Whenever someone wants out of a commitment, they start look

ing for a reason. Nettie began showing signs of discontent. She told her husband and young son that when she left, the child would have to stay with his father. Her reasoning was that the father was the better parent.

Nettie confessed to her husband that she felt trapped. She had jumped from one marriage into another, had a child, and bought a new home—but she had never given herself a chance to truly live. She was searching for a reason to get out of the commitment.

They discussed her feelings and agreed that if she left, their child would stay with the father.

As the story goes, Nettie finally met her Prince Charming at work. He was married with four children. He and his wife had what they called an "open marriage," meaning each partner engaged in extramarital affairs. He told Nettie this when they first met. It didn't bother her because, once again, she had fallen in love.

While still living at home with her husband and child, she kept the affair a secret. The change in her was obvious. She even told her husband she loved him like a brother.

Nettie eventually moved out and leased an apartment, which allowed her affair with Prince Charming to blossom. The husband had no choice but to file for divorce, understanding he would have custody of their son.

Nettie changed her mind and wanted custody. Prince Charming convinced her to fight for it, even though she didn't truly want custody.

It's sad that in many family court cases, custody is often awarded to the mother, regardless of whether the father is the more capable parent. When the divorce was finalized, Nettie was awarded custody.

It's not the size of the dog in the fight—it's the size of the fight in the dog.

The father had to fight relentlessly for his right to raise his son. This included hiring three different attorneys, going to court six times, and spending over $60,000. Each time he was denied, he got back up and kept fighting.

In the final custody battle, just weeks before Nettie and her new husband were set to take the child to Japan, a new judge presided over the case. After reviewing the evidence and hearing testimonies, he overturned the previous decision and awarded the father full custody.

This devastated Nettie. It wasn't just losing custody—it was that her attempts to destroy lives had failed. In the end, she destroyed her relationship with her only child. Her new husband also divorced her.

Today, she's just another zombie.

BÏR
ESTE

Well folks, I hope you've enjoyed the different characters you've just read. They came dressed to kill — and they did. Sometimes themselves. Sometimes the vibe. Always the illusion.

You've seen life as it struts in, high-heeled and hollow, and how quickly it slips into something... less comfortable.

This wasn't a tribute. It was a mirror held too long.
And in that reflection, you saw it — not just them, but maybe a flicker of yourself, too.
A hunger for more. For beauty, attention, immortality — even if it's in ruin.

But let's not mourn. Let's toast.
To cheekbones sharp enough to slice through denial.
To eyeliner that outlasted the lies.
To those who were never going to age gracefully, because grace was never the goal.

Although this is the end, it is the end of a new beginning that never ends.
In this house, no one ever really dies — they just fade into better lighting.

Stay tuned for the next Napoleon Esteban experience.
Because darling, the afterlife has a guest list.
And you're already on it.

www.ingramcontent.com/pod-product-compliance
Lightning Source LLC
Chambersburg PA
CBHW041142300726
48978CB00016B/1358